D1291711

Grandma Bumpheads

Patty Tate

Illustrated by David Anderson

 FriesenPress

One Printers Way
Altona, MB R0G 0B0
Canada

www.friesenpress.com

ISBN
978-1-5255-9638-4 (Hardcover)
978-1-5255-9637-7 (Paperback)
978-1-5255-9639-1 (eBook)

1. JUVENILE FICTION, ANIMALS, CATS

Distributed to the trade by The Ingram Book Company

Dedicated to

Larry

Kimberly, Megan, Whitney

Curt, Peter, Scott

Addison, Karson, Agatha, Logan

Mom, Mike, Dad, Ruth

My cup runneth over.

You may have tangible wealth untold;

Caskets of jewels and coffers of gold.

Richer than I you can never be-

I had a Mother who read to me.

from "The Reading Mother"
Strickland Gillilan

Agatha and Anastasia are cats.

Adventurous, creative, loving cats.

Agatha and Anastasia are sisters.

Agatha and Anastasia are different.

Agatha loves baseball.

Anastasia loves painted pawnails.

Agatha loves rock 'n' roll.

Anastasia loves the classics.

5

Agatha loves adventure stories.

Anastasia loves history.

EUREKA!

Agatha loves collecting rocks.

Anastasia loves collecting stamps.

But both Agatha and Anastasia love…

Grandma Bumpheads!

Ever since they could remember,
when Grandma came to visit,

she would lean in close and
touch her forehead to theirs.

Other relatives squeeze too hard or slobber wet kisses,

but Grandma Bumpheads just smiles her sweet smile and says, "Bump heads!"

If Agatha has a splinter, Grandma makes her feel better.

"Bump heads!"

If Anastasia has a fever, Grandma is the best medicine.

"Bump heads!"

12

If Agatha's report card needs improvement,

"Bump heads!"

If Anastasia's acting dreams don't pan out,

"Bump heads!"

The girls know that even if Grandma isn't there for teeter-totter mishaps,

leftovers,

14

hard landings,

and sold-out concerts,
they can always make
the best of things if
they just…

Bump Heads!

About the Author

Patty Tate has been a life-long believer that readers become leaders. Her childhood was filled with books, and she was blessed to have a mother that read all types of genre to her and her brothers. As an educator, Patty's goal was to instill the love of reading into each of her students. Whether it be through poetry, historical fiction and non-fiction, or the beloved Katherine Paterson novel, Bridge to Terabithia, she exposed her young charges to all manner of text. In 38 years of teaching, she was fortunate to share the love of reading with students from kindergarten to undergraduates in their respective college teaching programs.

   Patty received her Bachelor of Science in Elementary Education from Southern Illinois University in Carbondale, Illinois, and her Master of Science in Elementary Education from Southern Illinois University in Edwardsville, Illinois. She earned the distinction of becoming a National Board Certified Teacher in 2011. Patty lives in Carlyle, Illinois, with her husband Larry, where they raised their daughters Kimberly, Megan, and Whitney.